DINOSAUR PIRATES!

Triceratops

Allosaurus

Ankylosaurus

Iguanodon

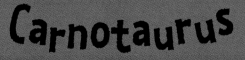

Carnotaurus

Megalosaurus

Stegosaurus

Baryonyx

Styracosaurus

Tyrannosaurus rex

For Caroline

First published 2016 by Nosy Crow Ltd
The Crow's Nest, 14 Baden Place,
Crosby Row, London SE1 1YW
www.nosycrow.com

ISBN 978 0 85763 583 9 (HB)
ISBN 978 0 85763 584 6 (PB)

Nosy Crow and associated logos are trademarks
and/or registered trademarks of Nosy Crow Ltd.

Text and illustrations copyright © Penny Dale 2016

The right of Penny Dale to be identified as the author
and illustrator of this work has been asserted.

A CIP catalogue record for this book is available from the British Library.

Printed in China

5 7 9 8 6 4

DINOSAUR PIRATES!

Penny Dale

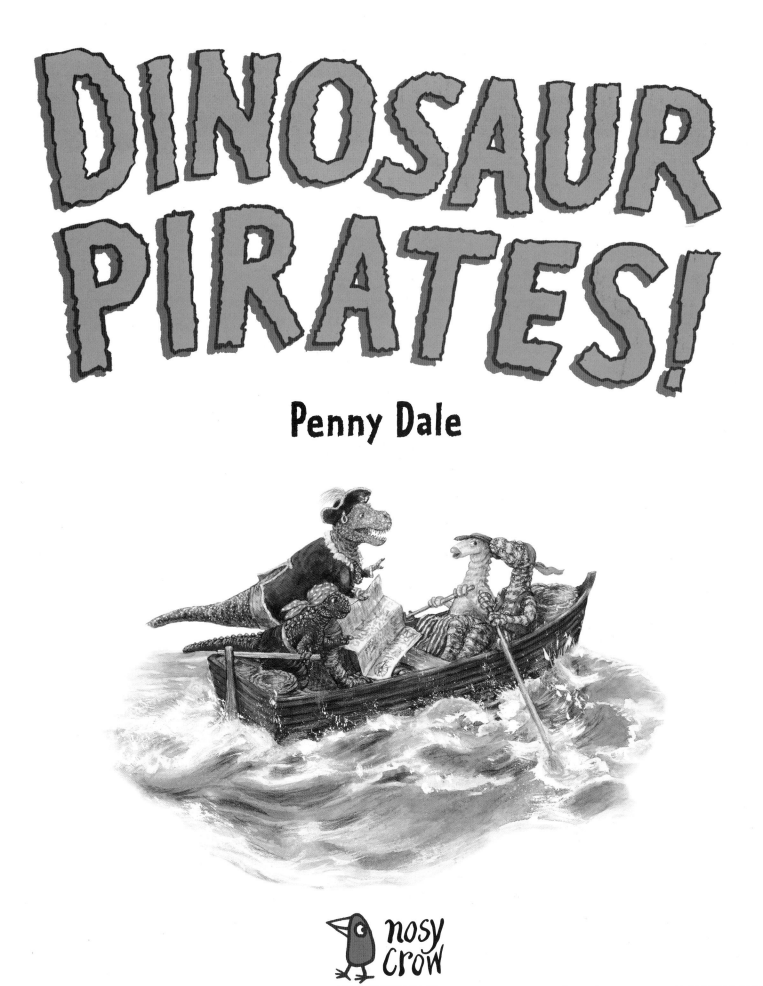

nosy crow

Pirate dinosaurs speeding,
speeding across the sea.
Across the sea,
in their sailing ship.

Creak!

Captain dinosaur planning, planning the secret journey.

The secret journey
to the distant island.

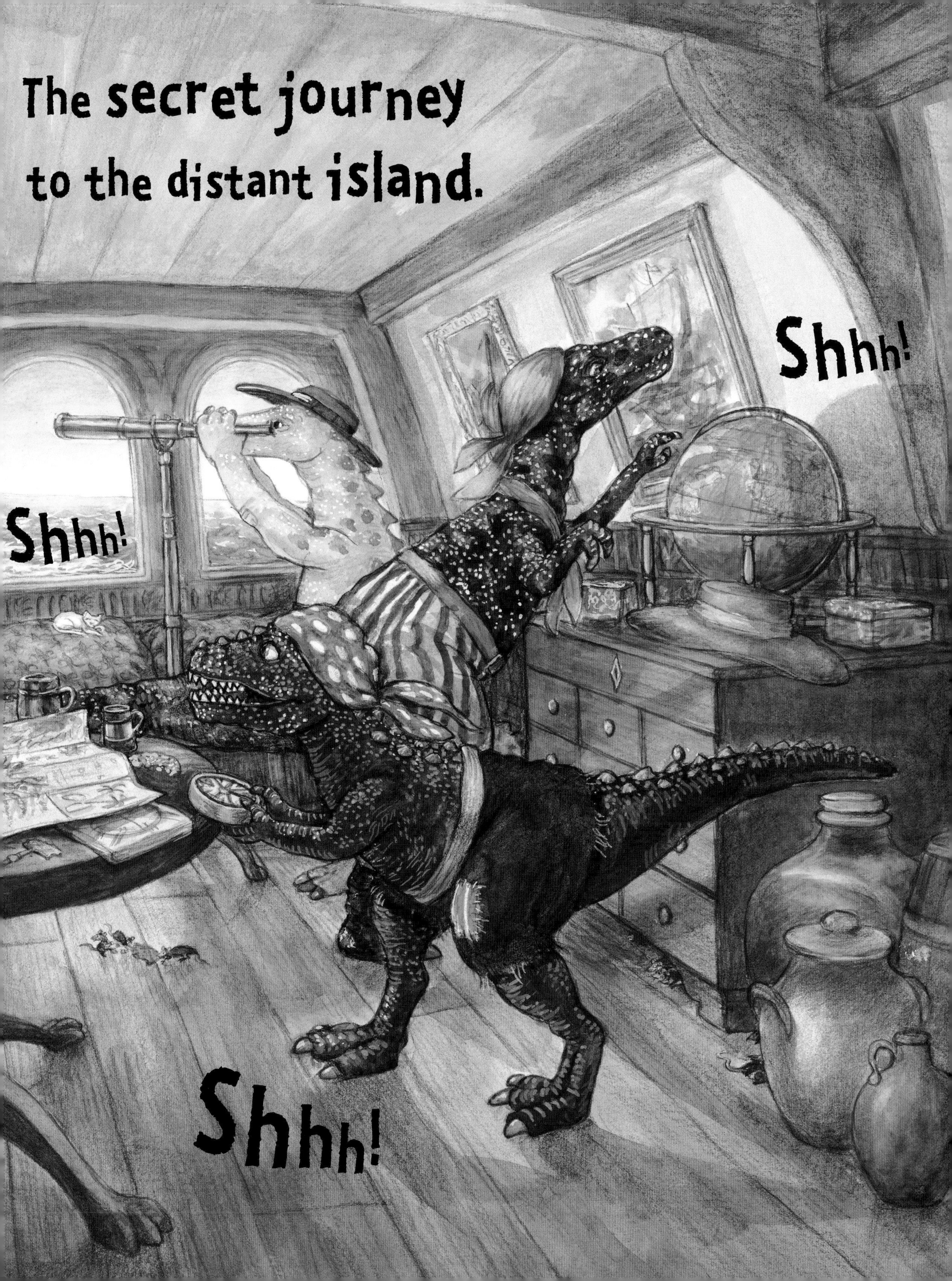

Busy dinosaurs working, working hard on the deck.

On the **deck**,
and up the **masts**.

Scrub!

Scrub!

Scrub!

Sleepy dinosaurs swinging,
swinging in
their hammocks.

In their hammocks,
till morning comes.

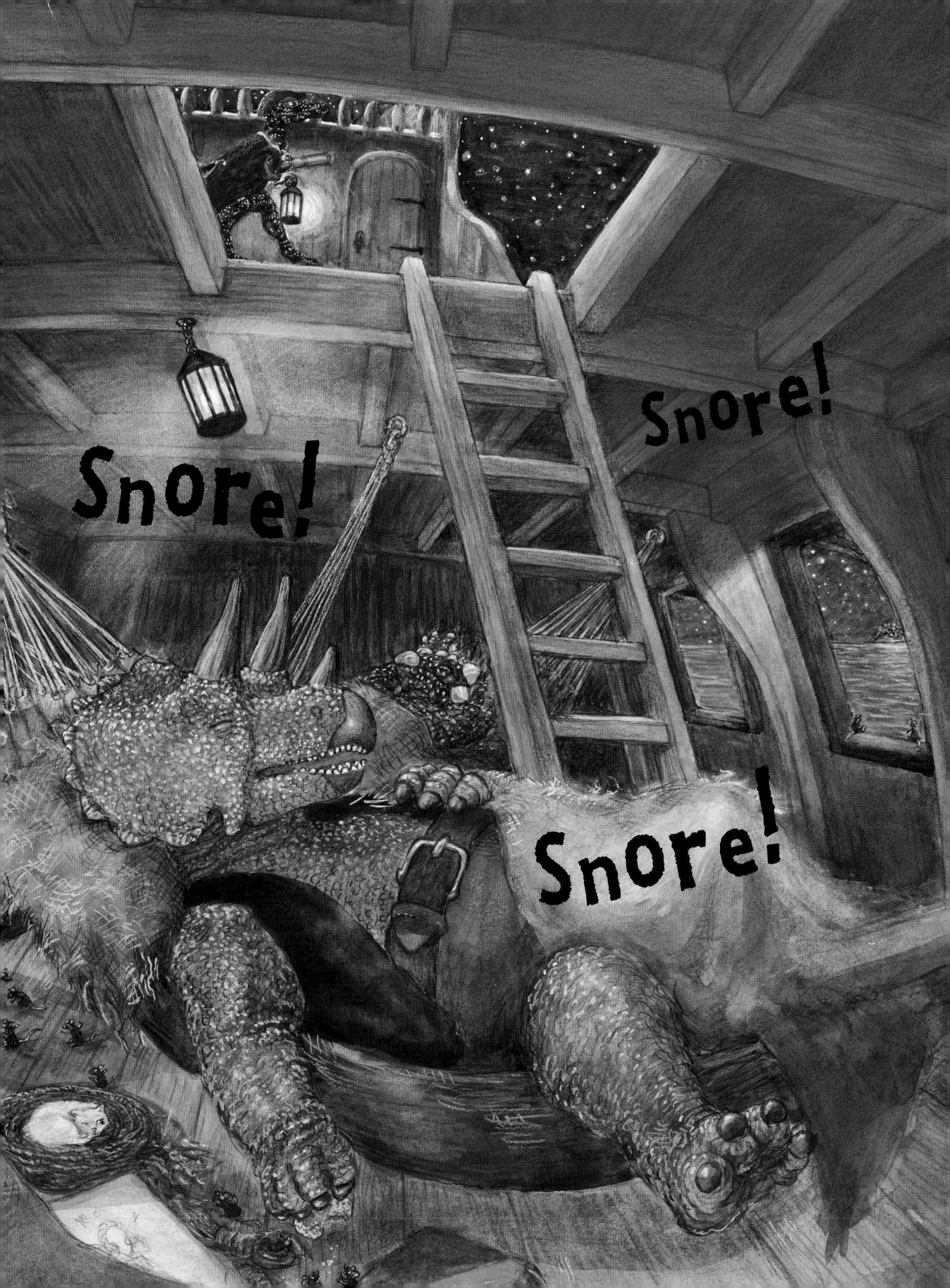
Snore!
Snore!
Snore!

Excited dinosaurs rowing,
rowing to the island.
The island on
the secret map.

Hot dinosaurs digging,
digging all day long.
All day long, until they find . . .
the treasure chest!

Heave ho!

Heave ho!

Heave ho!

Surprised dinosaurs roaring, roaring at the robber raptors.

Angry dinosaurs battling,
battling to save their ship.

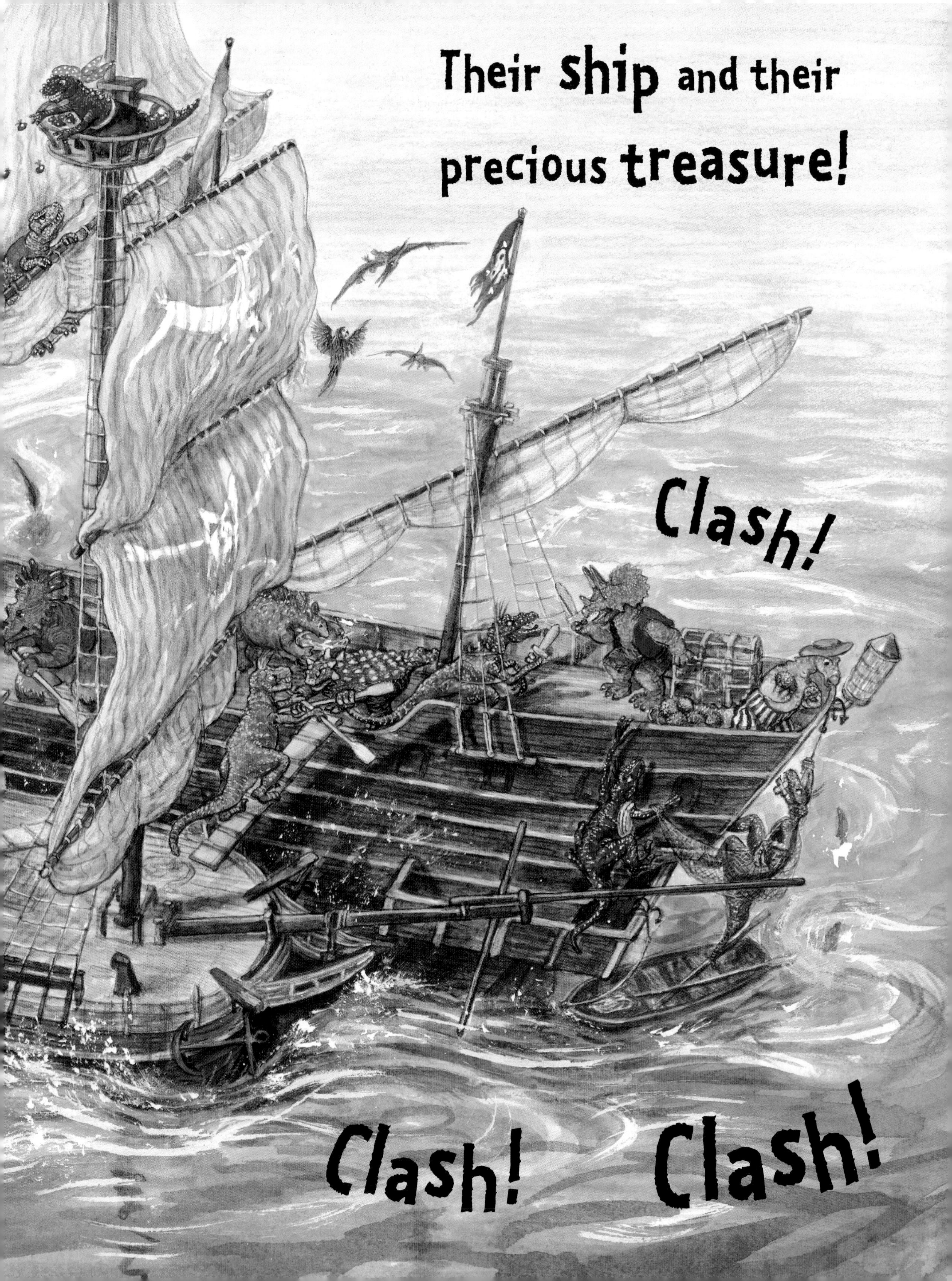

Their **ship** and their precious **treasure!**

Clash!

Clash! Clash!

Arrh! Arrh! Arrh!

Strong dinosaurs pushing,
pushing back the snapping raptors.
The snapping raptors,
whose ship is sinking!

Defeated raptors jumping,
jumping into the water.
Into the water and
swimming away.

Splash!

Splash!

Splash!

Victorious dinosaurs opening, opening their treasure chest.

Their treasure chest
that's full of gold!

Twinkle!

Twinkle!

Twinkle!

Happy dinosaurs dancing,

dancing and singing songs.
Pirate songs, all night long!

Jolly Roger

Lantern

Pieces of eight

Telescope

Pen and ink

Magnifying glass

Compass

Globe

Watch and chain

Map